Tales from the Canyons of the Damned

PRESENTED BY USA TODAY BESTSELLING AUTHOR
DANIEL ARTHUR SMITH

Tales from the Canyons of the Damned No. 23

First Edition

Special thanks to Jessica West

ISBN-13: 978-1946777591 ISBN-10: 1946777595

Cover By Daniel Arthur Smith

Horror Fiction from Holt Smith ltd
Agroland
Tower

For Susan, Tristan, & Oliver, as all things are.

A Brief Survey of Intergalactic Sports and Other Competitive Events

Will Swardstrom

WHEN IT COMES TO SPORTING EVENTS, Earth nations of the twentieth century believed themselves to be the center of the universe. Humans are frequently a bit short-sighted. There were some intellectuals who insisted the odds were too far in favor of other civilizations in the universe to be ignored, and some were just labeled crackpots for taking their pro-alien viewpoints to the masses. Of course, at the time, Earthlings thought there were no other intelligent lifeforms in the cosmos.

The universe might not have agreed that humans bore signs of intelligence in the first place.

However, we are not here to continue the debate over the competency of the human brain. Taking a look at those aforementioned twentieth century sports teams, we see examples of the "World Champion" Boston Red Sox or the "World Champion" Boston Celtics or the "World Champion" New England Patriots. On a side note, historians have disagreed as to whether any sports teams actually existed beyond the borders of Massachusetts in the United States of America.

Due to the sheer volume of information available vis a vis the American sports culture of the twentieth and twenty-first centuries, this article will generally steer away from discussions regarding those pastimes. Of course, as this is an article written for the descendants of the Great Earth Empire, we will endeavor to place the extraterrestrial sports in the context of Earth sports and culture.

(Author's Note: We would be remiss if we did not mention the brief foray by organized sports during the period now known as the *Z Era*, when humans believed a virus had mutated people into those dead but somehow still alive. Attempts were made by the unscrupulous to take advantage of this "apocalyptic" event by merging the stricken with the game of American football. But Z Ball, as it was dubbed, is an entirely different story. For an in-depth examination of that "sport," readers may wish to pursue articles which focus solely on the Zombie Football League.)

The Ciyaga are a species known to grow upwards of four meters (roughly thirteen feet) in height but are relatively thin and light compared to human beings. The atmosphere of their planet is what one would deem thin at best, with a climate producing storms that batter the three continental landmasses roughly every other day.

The Ciyaga are, of course, adapted to their environment, and their pastimes and entertainment reflect those adaptations—much like early Earth sports were adapted from skills needed to survive in a challenging environment.

Because of these weather systems, the Ciyaga can actually fly in certain conditions. Of course, the Ciyaga as a race have neither wings nor feathers, although they do have six appendages. Their length, the low gravity, and the otherwise inhospitable winds are the catalyst for a sport that would resemble kite flying on Earth.

In *Hol Folfal* (which translates to "Wind Rider"), ropes made from the hair of an indigenous herd animal are tied to the athletes, and they are launched—just as one would loft a kite—the day before a massive storm. Points are awarded for time aloft, degree of difficulty (wind speed, other environmental factors), and style. The coasts of the Ciyaga home planet are crowded with hopefuls taking advantage of the terrible conditions.

Of course, *Hol Folfal* is rooted in an ancient tradition, from a time when, to appease the gods, young Ciyaga were sometimes lofted in the days before and, indeed, during a storm. It was tragic, but the Ciyaga have credited this practice with cultural advancement among their people, as the sacrificed children frequently landed unharmed albeit hundreds of kilometers from home. As time went on, the Ciyaga learned to harness the wind for their own purposes and today, have a truly unified society due to the forced migration of their people.

The Apeck are a species few have heard of, because they are nearly impossible to see and communicate with—unless one happens to be the same size as an Apeck, of course. They have no home planet, but live near certain types of stars. They have no need of oxygen, an atmosphere at all, or the gravity generated by a planet.

Much of the life of an Apeck is spent in play, zipping around in the endless darkness of space. While scientists have had few opportunities to study the improbability that is the Apeck species, it is known that the closer the Apeck get to their chosen star, the slower they go. As they reach the apogee of their individual orbits around their sun, their speed reaches its maximum. The sport they spend the majority of their life pursuing perhaps most closely resembles distance running, if instead of twisting an ankle, one added the chance of burning inside of a sun to the possible consequences.

This journey around a sun is a race to the death, quite literally, for the Apeck. Interestingly, the winner of each race is not the one who survives. All Apeck are naturally drawn to the power, light, and warmth of the star itself, but the winner is the one whose essence first achieves oneness with the heavenly body they circumnavigate. To offer their own body and soul to become one with the star is the ultimate achievement, therefore, when the first competitor reaches the point of no return, the other Apeck drop away, allowing the winner to achieve oneness.

It is the ultimate sacrifice. Many Earth sports are imbued with themes of sacrifice. Historians can reference Kerri Strug in at the 1996 Olympic games, or Curt Shilling pitching for the Red Sox. Both cases were merely injuries to the lower appendage. Strug and Shilling lived full lives after their so-called sacrifices. The Apeck race might be more akin to the death of Dale Earnhardt, Sr. in a NASCAR race in 2001. A former champion, he died competing in, arguably, his sport's most famous race—on the final lap. The Apeck would recognize him for his greatness if any were able to stop long enough to learn what Earnhardt and NASCAR even were.

In that final moment before plunging into the heart of the star, the winner's body chemistry alters. Exobiologists are unsure as to how this process occurs: the event only takes place when the champion Apeck is too close to the sun to be observed at the microscopic level. The Apeck interacts in some form or fashion with the abundance of hydrogen to produce an effect that shoots out a rainbow of fire and sparkles. Observers have compared it to fireworks and the comparison seems appropriate.

While the Typpian race does not engage in willing self-sacrifice for the sake of their sport, they truly put their souls into it.

To understand the sport *Anam Gat* (which translates loosely to "Soul Golf"), one must first delve into the history of the Typpians themselves. The Typpian are a sentient race who perhaps most closely resembles albino squirrels found on Earth. Furry and small, the Typpian spent much of their ancient history living in burrows and caverns under the surface of their planet. It was only after the dominant species wiped themselves out through thermonuclear war that the Typpian emerged to make a life for themselves aboveground. Resulting both from Typpian heritage of underground dwelling and the massive wars that devastated their planet, there are countless holes leading to tunnels and caverns in every landmass.

Typpian lore harkens back to that time. It starts with integrating part of their body, which becomes the core of *Anam Gat*. When a Typpian dies, their body is treated and prepared in such a way that their heart becomes a mummified ball. The Typpians believe that by drying out the heart, they are preserving the soul of the deceased. And then, in a tradition that might appear to be callus to outsiders, the Typpian use this mummified heart as the ball in their game.

The Typpians take the mummified hearts and chase them around, beating them with sticks until each *Anam Gat* finds a resting place in their ancestral homes. In this way, they honor their dead *and* their history.

In some ways, *Anam Gat* resembles Earth's golf, but even human historians have pointed to the ancient civilizations of Mesoamerica. The Maya and Aztec civilizations sometimes played a game that required each team to advance a ball. The details of the games and rules are dramatically different from *Anam Gat*; the resemblance is in the construction of the ball. Sometimes the ball was manufactured from the rubber trees found on the Yucatan peninsula. More often, the ball was a skull encased in a rubber sheath. Generally, the skull was taken from the corpse of an enemy or the loser of a previous game.

In any case, the Typpian people have created a truly unique game from the ruins of a civilization now lost to time and history thanks to their first civilization's stupidity and greed. By embedding their very souls deep within the planet itself, the Typpian ensure that they remember their ancestors. And in a way, *Anam Gat* has ensured a bit of immortality for the Typpians as well.

Of course, humanity has long viewed itself as superior to all other races in the universe, even as evidence to the contrary mounted. From an objective point of view, it can be said that the prolific and extensive Yeitrian civilization, which emerged from the heavily populated planet Yeitr Prime, might be the most influential, and are therefore perhaps the greatest of all the civilizations in the galaxy. Through an accident of universal geography, the planet Yeitr Prime happened to be located quite near (galactically speaking) to a stable but shifting wormhole. The Yeitrians called this wormhole a *Contact Window*. It allowed them to be the first galactic explorers, much like that in the fictional Starfleet of Earth lore.

Many civilizations' first encounters were, whether by chance or on purpose, with the Yeitrians, so a vast number of the first documented records of these sports came from the annals of Yeitrian exploration.

Our next example of intergalactic sport comes not from those accounts, but from the record books of the Yeitrians themselves. While North American sports fans can point to the New York Yankee baseball teams or the University of Alabama Football teams as examples of dominance in their respective sports, the Iparraldoon *Zoine* team from the northern province of Yeitr may hold the record for consecutive winning seasons in a team sport.

Zoine is a sport that the Yeitrians borrowed from a culture they found via the Contact Window. Their time on this long-forgotten planet was brief but memorable. They had just enough time to witness the native sport when an asteroid slammed into the planet's moon, sending hundreds of streaking bolides at the planet, destroying the culture and people in one fell swoop.

It is not known if the Yeitrians truly fell in love with the game itself or whether, in their self-appointed role as the guardians of galactic cultures, they decided to adopt the game as their own. It is suspected that it may be the latter as the rules of the game have barely been adapted to accommodate Yeitrian physiology. The average Yeitrian is just two-thirds of a meter tall (about two feet), but the zoine (a sort of puck) used in the game is well over half that height. Unlike what is typically found in other civilizations, the object in play (the zoine in this case), is not proportional in any way to Yeitrian bodies, so it is logical to assume they simply used the same sized object as the previous culture. The only adaptation they appear to have made is the size of teams: thirty-three players take the court for each team during every play.

The rules of the sport are fairly mundane as team sports go, but the size of the puck and the massive teams involved make each game truly an example of entropy in action. As for the Iparraldoon team, they won forty-four of the first fifty league championship matches on Yeitr Prime, making them the standard-bearers for *Zoine* excellence.

Even today, it's hard to traverse the Yeitr solar system without coming across a planet with an Iparraldoon fan club. The sport has truly transcended its ignominious origins and become the dominant sport for what may be the universe's dominant civilization.

If the reader is a true intergalactic sports fan, then they have surely heard of Katsuo Imahara Johnson, the star player of the famed Saturn *Warexegon* (loosely translates to "Ring Race.")

Johnson is the latest in a long list of athletes to take part in the *Warexegon*, and the only current, and by far the most successful, human participant. Of course, the *Warexegon* is famed for being the most lethal individual sport in Earth's solar system since the American Football was outlawed in the late twenty-first century. The *Warexegon* is notoriously anti-human in its rules and how it is played. As viewers of the sport know, it is highly advantageous to have as many arms as possible. The Octirez dominated the sport in its early years due to their inherent assets.

The race is roughly 35 kilometers, and the athletes must cross the rings on foot (or corollary appendage) hopping from one solid ice chunk to another, while dodging rocks and other debris that make up the rings of the planet. The vastness of the planet and ring system, ensure each race is different. Rules were specifically designed to keep humans out, but for whatever reason, the game's commissioner never spelled out the anti-human bias in print.

Katsuo Imahara Johnson was raised on the Moon. He fell in love with the *Warexegon* and decided to take his chances, no matter what. Although Johnson has just two arms, his quick reactions allowed him to rise through the ranks. As he climbed, several of his rivals died in races and Johnson unexpectedly found himself the star of the *Warexegon*. Johnson might even be able to claim a higher level of fame than the President of Earth at this point in history, as his exploits have reached throughout humanity's colonies and beyond.

And perhaps *that's* the legacy that humanity has left to the universe when it comes to sports. In spite of everything, with obstacles and challenges meant to deter and even keep them away, humanity pushes forward, yearning to rise above. The glory and majesty of victory on the field of play is the ultimate lure for a human being. There is sacrifice, yes. Humanity is even known to sacrifice everything, reminiscent of the Apeck. The Typpian literally put their entire souls into their sporting endeavor, and humanity does the same. The story of Katsuo Johnson is a shining example of the best of humanity, for all other civilizations to see.

Johnson has famously said, "The *Warexegon* was like a siren, calling to me. It was a mistress I never knew I had or needed. Competing in this sport is the hardest thing I've ever had to do in my life, but I wouldn't trade it for anything. Not all the gold on the Moon. Come to think of it, I might be richer than all the gold on the Moon, anyway. I would do anything to play in the *Warexegon*. Anything. I suspect that I'll die competing, and they'll have to clean my body off the frozen ice around Saturn. The only ending I could ever want."

Sports fulfill a greater purpose than mere celebration. Some cultures pay homage to a more dangerous time in their ancient history. Some see it as a fulfillment of their entire being. Some honor the dead by honoring their sport. In Johnson, we see shades of all of those themes, and we believe there are other honorable underlying principles. Sports are a way that cultures reflect their past, showing who and what they honor in the process.

We'll conclude this analysis of sports in the cosmos with this quote by the legendary Tagr, a Yeitrian anthropologist, who upon seeing the Apeck race around a star for the first time, remarked:

"This sport… it is both majestic and horrifying at the same time. The sacrifice made by the Apeck in their final moments is awe-inspiring and in many ways, unfathomable. As someone on the outside, I cannot cognize the terror of burning up inside a star, but I was not meant to understand. This is a spectacle meant for one being and one being alone, and I will not deny them the glory they're due. I will simply bear witness and marvel their indomitability."

Tales from the Canyons of the Damned

Murder Bowl XIII

Nathan M. Beauchamp

ADRENOSPRINKLERS SHOWERED THE THRONG of fans swarming the stadium grounds with a red mist. I ducked my head and used a gloved hand to press my rebreather tighter against my face but still managed to get a taste of the stuff—sweet as sugar, salty as blood. It sent my pulse screaming like ripped sheet metal. I couldn't imagine what several lungfuls might do, maybe stop my aging heart cold. I moved with the chaotic flow of the revelers, scanning for signs of trouble. This was a fool's errand, one I wouldn't likely survive. But Slushii couldn't exactly bring his quantum hack here himself. He'd never make it into the arena. He'd been blacklisted from the biometric blockchain years ago. The MilPo would kill him the second he tested. Not that I'd last much longer. I could clear the blockchain, and Slushii swore his Golden Ticket would get me through the gates, but what then? I'd just as likely to get scrubbed out as succeed in uploading the hack.

A jumbotron glowed on the side of the stadium, bathing fans, tailgaters, and reporters in chartreuse-melon light. In the upper corner of the screen, a giant zero pulsed and crackled with the same rage and joy as the crowd. The murder ticker. Waiting for the first of the day. I felt it, eating into me, through my skinsuit, through the mask covering the wrinkles cut into my raw-skinned face. It hadn't been easy getting here from halfway across the country, and it wouldn't be easy staying hidden. Or staying alive once I made it inside the stadium.

As I watched, the digital murder ticker swapped out a zero for a one with exaggerated slowness. The crowd roared their approval, kicking in my sound-dampening earbuds, dulling the crescendo to a static hiss. The thump of celebration drums obliterated the announcer's voice echoing over the PA system. Nobody cared who'd bit it, just that someone—*anyone*—had. Murder Bowl XIII hadn't even started, but that first murder wetted the crowd's appetite and left them hungry for more.

The ticker quickly moved from two to three to four. The *pop-pop* of small arms fire from MilPo crowd control echoed over the concrete parking lot. Anyone shot dead for misbehaving wasn't counted on the ticker. Only genuine murders counted. Only the real fucking thing. If I somehow managed to make it inside the stadium undetected, install Slushii's transceiver, and release the hack, would they count the death of my target on that giant ticker of theirs? I doubted it.

In the nearest aisle of cars, a pair of teenage girls wearing see-through bras and electric collars played a flirty game of corn hole. Tossing bean bags toward the angled boards with cutouts for goals, they stretched and strutted, wiggling their asses, and made exaggerated pouty faces with rouge smeared across their cheeks. Their owner, a woman with some serious cyberwork covering the left half of her face, sharpened her broadsword with a whetstone. In front of her, a suckling pig roasted over a pothole filled with glowing charcoal. After several down strokes with the stone, she stopped and rotated the pig, then smiled up at me. "You want a taste?"

I wasn't sure if she meant the girls or the pig or both.

"No appetite," I said and meant it. I hadn't come to tailgate or fuck.

"Everyone's got an appetite," the woman said, smiling with chromed teeth, her face a dented trashcan lid. Her cybernetic eye strobed. A clumsy try at hypnotizing me? I might have worried, but my PPD—personal protection device—didn't register any serious security threats. The strobe was friendly, uber obvious. The hacks that work, you never see coming until you're choking on your own blood and vomit when a compromised subdural rips the side of your head open like a bloody volcano. She wasn't *really* hacking, just letting me know she could, if she felt like it. Her broadsword leaned against her knee, both of her hands where I could see them. One turned the pig on the spit, the other fondled the remote for the slaves' collars. I smirked. Cybers out the wazoo, augmens and top-shelf countermeasures, but the girl had a manual spit and a manual remote.

As if reading my thoughts, she grinned, ear-to-ear, eye now thumping along to the bass of the pregame drums. "Know what my dad used to say? If you want something done right, you sure as shit better do it yourself."

"Sure," I said, about to shove off. No time for chitchat.

Her eye pulsed. "He was right, you know." The cyber hefted her sword and ran her pinky along its edge, opening a pencil-thin line of red blood. She showed me the seep and smiled. "I killed him with this. My sixteenth birthday present. He was such a sweet old man. Stupid but sweet."

I'll bet he was. "I'm out," I said. "Going to check out the festivities."

"Two for one, if you want a ride," the cyber said, gesturing to the slaves. "Or *three* for one, if you're down…"

I didn't bother to answer, shambling away between the rows of vehicles, letting my PPD thermal scan the way forward. Long lines had formed at the gates, Golden Tickets glowing above the helmets of those who'd lotteried their way into a seat. I wasn't going to advertise my Golden Ticket yet. Nobody was supposed to bump a ticket holder, but that didn't mean it didn't happen. A fam of vloggers might let one of their lower-ranking members take the fall for waxing a ticket in exchange for the views. Poor sod would get dropped into a contest, eviscerated on live TV, then fed to one of the newly-bred bugs the lab boys were always cooking up. Like Napoleon said, a person will gladly die for a bit of ribbon. Or maybe a few million views.

Was that why I was here? The views? More than anybody ever got, if I pulled off this shit. But no, I didn't care about the views, at least not the way a vlogger like President Nick might. I wanted them, needed them, and hoped to hell I'd pull them, but not for me. For Sal. For my kid sis. That's why I'd come, almost a thousand miles, to the murder bowl. For Sal, and not one fucking thing else.

I hung in the shadows next to an abandoned purple and neon GangBang bus, watching replays on the nearest jumbo. Murder number one: a skinny kid in a motorcycle helmet split down the center by an ax. He'd strayed a bit too close to one of the professionals entering the arena and had paid the price. Murder two was a donation from the PepsiCoke Corporation—a little girl in a tutu dropped from a thirty-foot gallows. Her head popped off like a Champaign cork when she hit the end of the rope. That one had gone viral. Thirteen-million views and climbing. Three and four weren't even caught by the official streamers, but producers had cobbled together a chain of events using HeroCams and POV feeds. I watched it all, let it soak in through my facemask, into my eyeholes, into my brain. Numb. I'd taken a strong serotonin blocker before my arrival, and a neural balance stim. They'd keep me stable, stable enough to get the job done. If I got inside.

A lot of things needed to go right first.

Security was tight—no admittance without a ticket and leave your electropikes and hand cannons at the gate, thank you very much. I had my fake Golden Ticket at the ready and had come unarmed other than my PPD and the micro-transceiver loaded with Slushii's patch-n'-hack. I hung back until the lines thinned down and the murder counter had clipped past a hundred confirmed murders, each trying to outdo the last. I might have called it grizzly or demented or sick, but those words didn't mean much anymore. I sucked in a breath of mostly-clean air through the rebreather and beelined for the queue. Time to find out just how good Slushii's ticket really was.

Firing up my imager, a Golden Ticket popped into existence above my head, fuzzing at the edges where the cheap holo imager built into my headgear couldn't quite push it out with decent clarity. An intentional choice. Slushii thought of everything. Didn't want to look rich or important, just an average joe who gut lucky and won himself a front-row seat to the murder bowl.

"Fuck you, prick," someone shouted in my direction, but without a warning from the PPD, I didn't turn to see who it might be. I got my ass in line and thanked Big Pharma for the steady thrum of my heart, the lack of perspiration on my palms, the numbing numbness of not being able to freak, even if I'd wanted to.

"Hand in the scanner," the MilPo officer said, head encased in a shiny black helmet, exo suit humming, an electronic carapace. I removed the glove from my right hand and slid it into the imager sleeve. Light played over my palm, like one of those old office scanners back in the days of nine-to-fives and pension plans. Next came a little prick, and the suction sound of a tube whisking away a few milligrams of my blood. I was on enough meds and recreationals to seem like an average joe, but the blockchain processing took just long enough to make me start to feel whatever it is you feel when you can't feel nervous but should, by all rights, be fucking nervous. A ghost sensation, like a phantom limb.

"Endrick Giles," the Milpo said, reading the name on his screen. "Name sounds familiar."

I shrugged. "Fuck yeah, I'm a Giles. We're boss. Fucking righteous. You better know my name."

"Whatever, meat. Get moving," the MilPo said, then as an afterthought, added, "Enjoy the show."

"I'm stoked!" I said, feeling whatever it is you feel when you chemically can't feel relief.

I shot through the lines and lines of MilPo bug-suited security and up the ramp, into the stadium. I'm an old fuck, older than most, and can remember when stadiums hosted events that weren't about carnage and bloodletting. Before the first gladiator shows, then the gladiator teams, and the roll out of the New Olympics. Back when they threw around harmless balls (except to the animals who lost their skins to make them, maybe) and people bought overpriced hotdogs and beers and enjoyed some Sports Ball or whatever the hell they called it. I can just remember it, if I reach back to when I wasn't numb all the time, back to when it took a lot less than a kid getting brutally murdered to punch through the malaise and form a real, genuine emotion not bought off a shelf. I never went to one of those matches, but I've seen holos of them. Too slow, too boring, not enough human grist to grind, that's what people said. And so those old sports, they went the way of all things. Got themselves replaced by something hotter, sexier, harder, faster, more violent. Most violent. Because what's the cap on that? What's the upper limit? Where does it all just turn on itself and come burning to the ground like Caligula's Rome? I'm not smart enough to know the answer to the question. All I am is an old man with a clean history and biometrics that can pass the blockchain and the willingness to come here, to the murder bowl, to try and hold someone accountable for the shitstain of a country that we've become.

We don't have an emperor. Not in these, the Free United States of America™. We elect our despot, and we call them President. El Presidente to fifty-first through fifty-ninth states from the country formerly known as Mexico, but just President to the unlucky fucks living in the nuclear wastes north of our border. You know what sells even better than a good old-fashioned war? A nuclear war, where one side has them and the other side doesn't. Went off like you might imagine.

So now we're the Free United States of America™ and we stretch from the arctic down to the equator and fuck you if you don't like it. Let your opinion be known, and you'll get a first-class ticket to the Murder Bowl as a competitor. That's what they call you, but what you're competing for, nobody makes clear. In Rome, you had a chance, if you were good maybe, to win your way to something better. At the murder bowl, if you go out well (or especially poorly), you'll get some views, but that's about it.

Sal got a lot of views.

So many.

A bunch were me, watching my little sister catch fire, hair melting around her ears, the screams forcing her face into inhuman expressions of pain. Seared into my brain. There's a place deep down, deeper than Big Pharma can reach, and that's where she lives. My screaming horror of a sister. Burned to death. Hit sixty-million views and made a Greatest Of All Time compilation. She lives on where the stimulants and the suppressors and the levelers can't stimulate, suppress, or level. She's burned into me, and now, here I am, at the murder bowl, trying to make things right. Or at least less wrong, maybe.

My seat was near the forty-yard line, third-row back. Close enough to catch a stray arrow or magcoil round, to taste the acrid burning, to feel the wet slap of fresh blood. I got a much better view than President Nick, up in his secure skybox made of foot-thick acrylic and ceramics. The whole box doubled as a VTL (vertical takeoff and landing) and would whisk the bastard away at the first sign of trouble. AI pilot and security. Unhackable. So he watches from on high, and the crowd cheers, and when the last murder gets clocked and the ceremonies close, off he goes, back to the White House II.

I found my seat and squeezed in beside a male augmen at least seven feet tall wearing compression armor, his digital profile emitting military-grade security. I shaped my PPD around him, not wanting to get off on the wrong foot. The seat on my right remained empty until ten minutes before kickoff when another Golden Ticket arrived. A kid, probably fourteen or fifteen, geared out with branded merch from President Nick's vlogging fam.

"Can you believe this shit?" the kid said, shaking a shaggy-haired head, eyes glossy from whatever cocktail of drugs he'd taken beforehand. "Can you believe it?"

"No," I said. "I can't believe it."

"President Nick! He's up there! He's gonna do commentary for one of the quarters!"

"I've got it on preselect," I said. Not a lie. I wanted to hear President Nick's commentary. Twenty-one years old, golden-blond, movie-star beautiful, the President for the last two years, he'd come from a top-tier vlogging fam and had notched eleven kills himself in the runup to the last election cycle. Chief Nick, the youngest president in history. He'd invented the Golden Tickets lottery, and people loved him for it.

"He's a hero," the kid on my right said.

"He's my hero," I said, and the kid laughed—guessing my age, I shouldn't be talking like one of Nick's thirty-million vlog followers.

"Do you think we'll see bugs?" the kid asked.

"Probably—see the containment fields back there?"

"Hell yeah! Fuck. Fuck. Bugs. They fucking kill. You know what I mean? They fuckin' get at it. They're better than drones. Organics is where it's at, that's what I'm saying."

I needed to make it to halftime. That's when the President would address the crowd, the perfect time to release the hack. In the meantime, I'd have to listen to Nick's #1 fan rattle on about his favorite murders and which professionals he was going to cheer for.

"...unless they bring out the fucking bugs, and then I'm all bug, hundred-percent. Chomp 'em all, let's see it happen, first ever bug domination!"

Drones scare us because they're precise and emotionless. They scare our logical mind. Bugs reach deeper, down into the muck of our lizard brains. We evolved to fear them and the ones that come out of the labs...two-story primordial nightmares. Fat centipedes with titanium-enforced mandibles. Seventeen-foot-tall praying mantises. Swarms of dog-sized wasps that can turn your insides to pulp. They turn them loose on TV where conditions are controlled, but I couldn't see them pulling it off at the Murder Bowl, not with the space constraints. But fuck... If they did? Wouldn't that be something to see? A tinge of fear, down my spine like ice water. Fucking bugs. Couldn't take enough levelers to stop that from reaching deep.

"All rise for the national anthem!" the PA blared.

We stood. Or most of us did.

A woman in the upper levels, slow on the uptake, took a mascot's sniper round to the cranium, blowing out the back of her head into the surprised fans behind her. Cheers erupted, and the murder ticker slid one higher. Fans couldn't murder other fans, but the mascots had free reign to take out anyone they liked to keep things fresh.

The anthem played, and Nick waved from the jumbotrons, surrounded by topless girls—

One of which was Secretary of State Maddison Rivers, famous for the anal scenes she'd shot with Nick before securing her nomination.

Jets rocketed overhead. Fireworks exploded. An intentional misfire landed in the upper deck—the cheap seats came with certain risks—and burned a couple families to ash. More cheering. I closed my eyes, remembering Sal. The pain still lingered, despite trying to scratch it out with whatever I could get my hands on. Would today help? Would it? If I didn't make it out, the pain would go along with me. Maybe.

Fucking President Nick sent a stream of the burning carnage from the upper deck out to his fans, views climbing by tens of thousands a second. Napalm-infused letters crackled over the video of the murdered fans: "EAT MORE FRIED CHICKEN!"

The murder ticker had hit almost four-hundred by kickoff.

I stood when expected, cheered when expected, high-fived the teenager when expected. Numb. I was numb. I'd always been numb. Leveled out. Nothing touched me. Not when a bus of dissident children got torn apart by backhoes with sharpened scoops. Not when teams of professionals charged in and finished the job, toddlers on pikes like skewered olives waiting to go into a martini glass. Not when blood spurted over the crowd, over me. Halftime. I was here for halftime, and I was numb, and I didn't care about the bugs eating human bodies, the electronic hum of the containment fields frying the bugs to cinders once they'd finished the job. I couldn't hear the crowd screaming, couldn't see the looks on my fellow human's faces, those dumb enough not to wear head gear. I didn't see it, I didn't hear it, and I absolutely didn't *taste* gunpowder, sweat, napalm, tears.

Halftime.

It took me a moment to stand, legs wobbly. Rattled, more than expected, more than I should have been, considering I had work to do.

"Fucking amazing!" The kid next to me lit the bowl of a pipe and inhaled crystal. "Did you see the fucking bugs?"

"No, I'm blind," I said, pushing past him, ignoring his confused expression.

The murder ticker climbed steadily; fans not lucky enough to have a ticket going at it outside the arena and fans inside picked off by one mascot or another. A few breaking the rules, taking each other out, instigators taken by MilPo to the lockers, prepped to "compete" in the second half.

Fucking numb. That's what I wanted to be, what I should have been. Numb. Leveled. Ready to do my job. Below, staff cleared the field for the halftime show. Rumors crackled over the socials that Nick might fuck someone live on stage. Fuck them, kill them, what difference did it make?

The transceiver took some effort to get out, even with me squatted over a toilet, pushing hard. At last it fell, then I plucked it out of the water and wiped it clean with a wad of toilet paper. The things Slushii made me do. The parts he cut out of my mind, the parts he added so I would match the profile of the original owner of my Golden Ticket. Those parts are inside me now, and they like what they've seen, like the whole fucking show. Succeed, and they'll be inside me still. Maybe. If I survive. If I want to survive.

The transceiver wasn't much to look at and smelled like shit. I turned it on and plugged it into a network socket in one of the food stalls. That's all it took, Slushii told me. It felt too easy. The transceiver powered up, formed a network connection, then spooled out the hack through the wireless access points connecting to fan's subdurals. Adhocking them into a neural network. Too easy. But Slushii was a genius. He perfected quantum, hidden away from view, off the radar. An artificial intelligence, the first of his kind. About to show the world what quantum could do with its fancy superpositions. Normal code, normal computing, uses bits that are either a one or a zero. Its' called binary because it's just that— one thing or another. Quantum fucks with the paradigm. It uses ones and zeros, "on" and "off," but throws in a one that's also a zero. Or maybe it's zero that's also a one. They call it a superposition, not that I'm an expert.

President Nick took the stage. He ripped off his silver track suit. Naked, dick erect, arms raised, crowd cheering him on. President Nick didn't create any of this, he was just another reveler. Killing him wouldn't change *this*. Would it? Maybe not. But he was going to pay. For Sal. His subdural exploded, lancing off his left ear, ripping his facial skin free of the bone beneath. His left eye, an empty cavity. He screamed in confused fury as the containment fields collapsed, freeing the rest of the bugs.

Slushii thought of everything. The hack wasn't quantum. It just opened the doors. Every connected device became a little portal letting Slushii in, pulling his data over the networks, through socials. From the secret laboratory, breaking down the blockchain, breaking down, well, *everything*. There's no such thing as encryption to Slushii. Something, something, network effect. Something, something, nodes. I don't remember it, I do remember it. Maybe.

The murder ticker skyrocketed, then fuzzed out. The stadium went dark. Screams filled the smoke-filled concourses. The bugs were loose. One eviscerated what was left of President Nick. Far more scrambled into the stands, pushing even more fans into the packed concourse.

I crouched in the food stall, watching fire lick melting plastic cups still coated with beer froth. Sal burning. Was that a part that Slushii added? Or did he take some part of it away? I can't remember. I can remember. Until the thought is formalized, understood, can't it be both? Sal alive, Sal helping create Slushii. Sal naming him after a DJ named after a desert. Sal still alive, back at the secret lab. Or Sal gone, her murder watched sixty-million times. She was alive. She was dead. She was both.

Echo Dome
Bob Williams

"SHIT." DIAMOND SLIDES THE CUFF of his rain gear off his wrist and glares at his chrono for at least the third time in who knows how many minutes. The air-trans is late, and he fears the client is gonna be pissed. He doesn't want to deal with crap. Because if the client gets pissy, Diamond gets pissy, and the nice little business arrangement he has lined up will not come to fruition.

His four and half foot tall, three bills heavy frame takes up a good bit of space under the covered porto. Good thing he's the only one there. He drags heavily off the butt that hangs from his lips, the embers consistently slithering closer the filter. He flicks the butt out into the rain, expelling the smoke out through his nostrils, and starts to pace.

Luckily, one trip to the end of the porto is all that's required. The hovering sound of the air-trans draws near when he makes the turn back. He quickly strides to the arrival zone and does his best to not look agitated. No easy feat, especially considering his usual 'intimidating' demeanor. He lights another smoke and reaches into the interior pocket of his rain gear to extract the paperwork.

He unfolds the collection papers as the mist from the falling rain eats away at the edges. Diamond takes two steps back. He quickly scans the low dome one last time.

"Okay, Mr... Ranger," he says. "Let's make some money."

The air-trans hovers into the arrival zone and locks into the dual clamps. Once the red light shifts to green and the "all clear" claxon sounds, the rain defense extends from the transit and docks to the porto. Diamond brought extra-fortified rain gear just in case the Ranger-asshole hadn't heeded the warnings about the rain.

The door hisses loudly, then shifts from left to right, revealing the lone traveler of the evening. Diamond chokes down a laugh. Mr. Ranger stands five foot plus a dick head tall, and weighs maybe a hundred and thirty five pounds in his black suit, black shirt, and black tie.

Diamond approaches in a non-threatening manner, with both hands out and open, and summons as much of a smile as he can muster with the smoke dangling from the corner of his mouth. In reality, he already wants to slap this bitch and he doesn't even know him. But... *Hanson said he was legit, so I'm gonna treat him like it's so.*

"Mr. Ranger—" says Diamond.

"Just Ranger," he interrupts. "Diamond, I presume."

He shrugs. "Just Ranger it is. Follow me, please. I have sec-trans right this way. Did you adhere to the rain stipulations? If not, I have the appropriate gear, sir. Courtesy of Hanson."

Ranger reaches out and accepts the rain kit, tucking it under his arm, and continues to walk.

"Hold on, Mr. Ranger. You see I'm *wearing* my gear, right? This isn't a free fuckin monogrammed robe at an overstay, man. Do not tussle with this rain, Russell. You feelin' me, man? Go ahead and put it on. I'll wait."

He does.

"Good. Now let's get shakin'."

"How soon will I be sitting down with Hanson?"

"Look, Ranger, Hanson wants me to show you a good time. There's plenty of time to meet up with the boss man."

"What do you mean, a good time?"

"Well," says Diamond. "I'm talkin' 'bout the Echo Dome."

"Mr. Diamond—" Ranger begins.

"Just Diamond," he interrupts.

Rangers flashes a wry smile and nods. "Diamond, Strickland has given me express orders to conduct our business transaction with Hanson and return to the sector immediately."

"And that's all well and good, Ranger, but Hanson, who's *my* boss and whose sector you're currently in, wishes for you to take in a little entertainment in our fair sector. Would you say that you understand what I'm telling you? Or do you speak another language in your fuckin' sector?"

Ranger steps into Diamond's personal space and looks him dead in the eye. "I understand you just fine. I will go with you to this 'Echo Dome.' Then we will conduct our business, and I will explain to Hanson how completely dissatisfied Strickland is with our treatment here, and we'll see how your business responds afterwards. So please, lead the way to your secure transport."

"Sec-trans awaits. Follow me, please."

The two men ride in silence, the steady rain the only sound. Ranger fidgets and says, "Diamond, I offer my apologies for my outburst. I'm nervous. Honestly, I've never left my sector. To coin an ancient phrase, I'm a fish out of water."

"Not in this rain, you're not. We're all fish here," says Diamond. He expels a large plume of smoke into the dash vent.

"Well. I am sorry. Let's begin again, shall we?"

"Sure thing. Forever forward, as they say."

"Agreed. So, what exactly is an 'Echo Dome'?"

"Well… The sciency robot shit is way over my head. All you need to know is, if you think you can judge a man just by lookin' at him, you'll go broke faster than a sunny day in this fuckin' sector."

"That's not actually telling me very much."

"Sit tight, Ranger. I'd never lead a client astray. Especially one who's got a deal lined up with Hanson. We'll be at the dome shortly, and you'll see it all for yourself." He turns to face Ranger. He squares up on him. "I really hope you can handle the dome, my friend. It's been known to strip a man."

Ranger swallows. "Strip a man?"

"Of his very soul."

Diamond deposits the vehicle in a secure location arranged by Hanson. No one with a brain in their head would touch his transit. He collects his belongings, including a wad of currency from the locked middle console, and flips the broad hood over his head. "You got gloves? Eyewear?"

"No," says Ranger.

Diamond shakes his head. "Okay. We're gonna have to be quick then, but the dome's not far. Flip up your hood. Far as you can over your head. Don't pull the strings, man. Let the overhang cover your eyes. Keep your head down. Dig those hands deep in your pockets. Only take 'em out if your hood blows off. Got it? We'll land you some specs inside."

"Fuck," grunts Ranger. "How do you people live in this shit?"

"Carefully. Now, let's go have some fun. No weapons. Okay? Open up, double over, and stay close."

Raucous cheering penetrates the walls, even above the rain, the instant they leave the trans. Synthesizers key hard notes and strobe lights pulse in what looks like a prehistoric strand of DNA encompassing the dome entrance. Not a formidable building, it's a mid-sized auditorium with a domed roof.

Diamond claps Ranger hard on the shoulder and shoves him through an L-tech weapon locator. Once they both clear, Diamond reveals his forearm barcode tattoo. After it is scanned and cleared, he notifies the attendant his client doesn't have a tat, pays the correct currency, and they're in.

Ranger grabs Diamond's arm and turns him around. "You still haven't explained what we're doing. What are we going to see? What the hell is going on?"

"Shit, Ranger, you all right, man? You look like you scraped a brick on the sly. You can't be using other product before Hanson's. Your fuckin' head'll explode."

"I haven't sampled any product. I'm the currency on this arrangement. I'm simply asking, again, for clarification about what we're doing."

"Gambling. We're fuckin gambling, man," says Diamond joyfully.

"Gambling? On what?"

"Humanity."

Diamond and Ranger make their way into the atrium of the building where people are milling about. "There aren't that many citizens here," Ranger says. "And, hey, this building is a piece of garbage. It's not far from being condemned."

"It's the rain. Soon as this building rots, it'll just move to the next one."

"Hanson had you bring me to an underground fight ring? Come on, Diamond! I can guarantee you this is not my thing. Let's get back to the trans and go meet Hanson."

"Eh. Take a deep breath, Ranger. I can guarantee you, you ain't never seen anything like this. Follow me. We need to see who's on the card and throw some currency their way."

Ranger follows closely behind with his head on a swivel.

The raucous roars aren't coming from the people inside. Ranger assumes more will show up right before the bell. Like most combat venues. There are large monitors protruding from the walls throughout the atrium, which is a massive area, round in diameter, able to hold triple the amount of the current citizens.

All monitors broadcast the same screen. There are four columns.

FIGHT #1	FIGHT #2	FIGHT #3	FIGHT #4
CLOSED	CLOSED	CLOSED	OPEN
WINNER:	WINNER:	WINNER:	FAVORED:
PITBULL	HARBINGER	HACKSAW	ONE SHOT > BREAKER

Ranger studies the list, and Diamond claps him on the back, hard, for a second time.

"Fuck yeah! One Shot!" Diamond shouts, his arm slung around Ranger as if they were lifelong friends. He pumps his fist into the air.

"You know this 'One Shot'?"

"No, but with a name like One Shot, I can feel the currency raining down on me," Diamond laughed.

"I'll take that action. I'll take Breaker with the upset for all the currency on your person."

Diamond stares at him in silence before erupting in a high-pitched cackle. He laughs for nearly a rotation.

"Deal," he says, "and copy back. All the currency on your person."

"It's set."

"My man. You have no idea what you're about to see. Let's hustle up and get inside. You don't want to miss the intro, newbie."

The two men from opposite sectors walk side by side down the long corridor which looped around a corner and into the arena. A mammoth four-sided jumbotron hangs from on the top of the dome on thick metal poles, and screens decorate the wall along the entire inner circumference of the Echo Dome.

"Diamond? The dome isn't *that* big. What the hell are all these screens for?"

Diamond pulls back the sleeve of his rain gear and sees their seat numbers blinking directly over the barcode tattoo on his forearm. Simultaneously, the overhead lighting blinks up and down three times.

"Follow me. Your mind is about to be blown," he says.

Diamond and Ranger make their way to their seats and get situated just as the lights dim to complete darkness. The general carousing of the crowd, which has grown dramatically in size, disperses in a synergy that travels around the circular arena like falling dominoes.

Suddenly, two high-wattage spotlights focus on an octagonal cage in the center of the arena. Next, all of the widescreen monitors cut on in succession, all flashing the same message:

WELCOME TO THE ECHO DOME!!

Brilliant strobe lights flash and wave throughout the darkness as nearly ear-piercing techno music and powerful beats rock the house.

Diamond pokes Ranger hard with his elbow. "Here comes Mr. Show. I'm sure you get what his job is." The two spotlights remain focused on the cage, but a new spotlight targets a door on the far wall of the dome. The music and flashing lights stop.

The door flies open and slams against the wall as the crowd erupts in a cacophony of cheers. The strobe lights, techno music, and pumping beats begin anew as Mr. Show stands marvelously in the spotlight.

Mr. Show swaggers toward the octagonal cage. Waving his arms in a *louder, louder* motion while strutting charismatically in time with the beat. The man is a performer, and the insane citizens in Echo Dome are his rapt and willing captives. For the moment.

The third spotlight follows Mr. Show as he makes a production of unlocking the cage and walking slowly to the center. Once there, he waves his arms in incitement once more. Begging, the crowd raises their voices in boisterous anticipation of what is about to occur.

With both hands raised slightly above his head like an ancient orchestral conductor, Mr. Show…waits…waits… then hypnotically lowers them to his hips. The strobes, the lights, the beats, and the people all succumb to total silence in the moment.

Two spotlights disappear, leaving a single spot shining straight down upon him. Without a word, he takes the index finger of his right hand and swipes the barcode tattoo on his left forearm three times. Every monitor in the dome simultaneously connects, cuts on, and broadcasts the face of Mr. Show. He then draws two intersecting rings over the barcode tattoo and the pop of a public address system goes live.

"Ladies and gentlemen, welcome to… THE ECHO DOME!!! Zeta sector's only noncontact echo-combat arena. And the premier echo-combat destination in *ALL* of the Omega Quadrant." The crowd boos as part of the ritual. "Ah, shut the hell up, you bloodthirsty wackos! Mr. Show knows! Yes he does! Mr. Show knows exactly why you're here tonight. Complete and total psychological and emotional devastation! Fuck yeah! Am I right? Mr. Show always knows!"

The crowd roars with delight.

"Noncontact?" Ranger says. "What the…"

"Shut up, man. Just watch and listen."

"For all newcomers to the Echo Dome, a brief explanation of what you are about to witness. For the rest of you, just shut up and be patient. The Echo Dome's noncontact echo-combat is ingenuity at its finest. Created by a mechanical engineer named Dr. Braden Ghall, combatants are given gloves, for lack of a better term, for both hands and feet. The hand gloves have electronic sensors for all four knuckles of each fist. The foot glove has one larger sensor that rests directly below the toes. Those are for striking.

"On the receiving end, combatants are given a halo band with four small yet powerful receptors. For the upper body, a virtually skin-tight, flesh-colored shirt with a large receptor over the sternum, and four more on the shoulders and elbows respectively. Below the waist, there are sensors on the hips, thighs, and calves. Echo-combat is completely noncontact.

"When a strike 'lands,' it means a sensor has come within one-half inch to six full inches from a receptor. Once that occurs, a coded message travels to the halo itself, which then sends a very concentrated electric pulse to the cerebral cortex, triggering an echo. A memory. When an echo causes a combatant to surrender, their opponent wins. If there is not a submission prior to a fifth echo, the match is not only a draw, but both combatants are banned from the Echo Dome for life.

"Understand all that, newbies?" Mr. Show yells. "Combatants in my Dome have to be nasty. Have to be mean. Have to be cruel. Have to be calculated. But most importantly, they have to be guarded."

Diamond turns to Ranger. "You get it now. Some of the echoes—man, they're ten times worse than any bloodbath street fight you've ever seen. Echoes are life, man. Everything you'll see on those screens has actually happened."

"How have I never heard of this? This is unbelievable!"

"Well, it's not exactly legal. Sec-Gov just tends to stay away from it, at least here in our sector, because since echo-combat came to this sector, crime as a whole has gone down."

"You're telling me the Echo Dome is a crime deterrent?"

"Yeah. But they don't outright legalize it 'cause there are plenty of saps that get their eggs scrambled permanently. I saw this guy one time go fuckin' straight catatonic right in the middle of the cage, man. No shit."

"And now," says Mr. Show. "It's time for the main event! Bring out the combatants." Two new spotlights appear at opposite ends of the dome as two gates roll aside to present the competitors. The music and pageantry fire up again as the men jog to the cage. Once Breaker and One Shot enter the octagonal emotional war zone, everything stops almost faster than it started.

"Ladies and gentleman!" The crowd explodes once again in an uproarious fashion. "Welcome the Echo, Echo, Echo... *DOOOME*!!!" Tonight's combatants come from opposite ends of the spectrum. One man is a ferocious, well-established beast. The other, a first timer to the Echo Dome with nothing but exceptional psychological and emotional pre-scores."

"Citizens, I give you the undefeated, mentally fortified wall of shattered psyches, One Shot!" The crowd takes their frenzy to another level for the established veteran of the dome. "His opponent, well I don't know shit about him, but here he is—Breaker!" The dome went so quiet, a bead of sweat could almost be heard hitting the dome floor.

"Okay, okay, you turds!" screams Mr. Show. "Your referee for tonight's contest is Jesus. You know what that means, gentlemen. You better pray this doesn't end in a draw. Now, come to the center of the cage."

Mr. Show leaves the cage as the combatants meet in the middle. They shake hands. One Shot and Breaker are separated only by Jesus, who swipes his barcode tattoo twice in rapid succession to activate his public address microphone.

"One Shot," he says. "Are you ready?"

One Shot stands six feet four inches tall. He weighs two hundred and sixty-five pounds. His head is shaved, his face shows a week's worth of beard, and his body is lean. He looks angry. He looks confident. He looks ready for combat.

"Yes."

"Breaker. Are you ready?" Jesus asks.

Breaker stands five feet six inches tall. He has a styled haircut and looks so smooth, one might confuse him for a model if you were to see his face from under his rain gear. He is toned to an above-average but not exceptional level. He looks terrified. He doesn't look like a skilled combatant. But he does look determined.

"Yes."

"All right, gentlemen, your sensors and receptors have been checked and are working properly. No physical contact. Protect your thoughts at all times. Return to your corners and begin combat when I signal. Good luck."

The two combatants glare at each other briefly before returning to their respective sides of the cage. The Echo Dome is a vacuum. But for a new bank of lights encompassing only the octagonal cage, all remaining environmental functions go dark. All the fanfare from mere moments ago is gone.

"Combatants! On my mark. Three... two... one. Begin!" He brings his hands to together in a thunderous clap, then retreats several steps to officiate the combat.

"Come on, One Shot, you son of a bitch! Come to Poppa. Bring me that currency!" howls Diamond, practically frothing at the mouth.

One Shot and Breaker meet in the center of the cage, nodding respectfully before backing and away and beginning the competition. The next several minutes is a veritable ballet of head fakes, half punches, and semi-kicks. Not a single strike is attempted.

"What the hell are they doing?" Ranger shouts.

"Ranger, my man. Stick with it. Zero in. You aren't going to see anyone get hit here. Got it? So how close you miss is critical, man. Echo-combat is precise, articulate, and masterful. We've come out of the cave, Ranger. We don't drag women around by their hair and hit people with sticks. This isn't boxing, where you might see two-hundred punches in twelve rounds. In this very fight, you might see only two strikes land. It only takes one echo and it's over."

The two fighters continued to jockey around the cage. Breaker throws a straight front kick with lightning quickness. One Shot catapults backwards, avoiding the strike, then closes the space between and counters with a fake of the left before bringing the right fist around uninhibited. The hairs on One Shot's arm stand erect all way to his shoulder as all five sensors register on Breaker's left temple receptor.

Mr. Show barks over the public address system. "Strike recorded! One Shot. Echo forthcoming, Breaker." The combatants return to the corners. The crowd quietens.

"You never forget your first echo. No matter what you see." Diamond whispers. "Check it out, Ranger! Here it comes." Rangers stares intently at the large screen.

ECHO FORTHCOMING: BREAKER
ECHO FORTHCOMING: BREAKER
ECHO FORTHCOMING: BREAKER

The screen comes to life:

Three hooded figures stand poised in front of a chain-link fence. A damp mist blows left to right, casting a red-blue hue from the neon lights of next door's industry. The middle figure steps forward, approaching the gate's security scanner. He slides his protective goggles up to his forehead and begins fishing into the pocket of his rain gear.

"Come on, come on!" says another of the figures. "Hurry up, goddamnit. We don't have all night, Johnny!"

"I know, I know." He continues to dig. "Ah ha!" The figure pulls out a flat metal card from his pocket. No bigger than three by three inches, the card has a series of numbers stamped into the metal. He wipes the card on his pant leg so it's as dry as possible, then pulls the sleeve of his rain gear back and places the card over the barcode tattoo on his forearm. Once the data transfers to his barcode, the man places his tattoo under the scanning laser, and the gate opens.

All three whoop as the gate easily slides open to the air-trans dealership. The two other criminals take off, leaving the man who opened the gate alone. He stands motionless for a moment before striding confidently onto the grounds and across the lot to a particular vehicle.

It's resonant shiny purple with gold racing streaks down the side. He exposes the barcode once again and draws two intersecting triangles before putting his hand on the door handle, waiting a moment, then opening the door. He slams the top of the car with max volume and yells, "Let's go! Now!"

He unlocks all the doors, and before he can start the air-trans, his friends arrive. He turns to his friend in the front passenger seat who still has his goggles down. "You ready to ride this bitch 'til we can't ride it no more?

"Hell yeah!" He cackles as he says it. The friends share glances at each other before the vehicle is started with the push of a button.

On all four sides of the massive jumbotron, a smiling, laughing face reflects off a pair of rain goggles. It's Breaker.

"He's a thief," Ranger says, turning to Diamond. "He stole an air-trans."

"No shit. Not everybody's first echo is a murder, man."

"Breaker!" booms Mr. Show. "Your echo is public. Do you wish to concede?"

"No," replies Breaker with conviction.

"Very well." Mr. Show turns to Jesus. "Carry on."

Jesus activates his PA system. "Combatants, begin on my mark!"

On the sound of the clap, One Shot and Breaker meet once again in the center of the cage and nod.

Before Breaker could even blink, One Shot lands a lightning fast leg strike to his calf sensor.

"Strike recorded! One Shot. Echo forthcoming, Breaker," shouts Mr. Show.

ECHO FORTHCOMING: BREAKER
ECHO FORTHCOMING: BREAKER
ECHO FORTHCOMING: BREAKER

The jumbotron snaps to life.

A faucet runs continuously. Hot water causes steam to cover the mirror, concealing the identity of the figure standing before it. A hand swipes across the mirror several times, revealing Breaker. He's no more than fifteen years old. He's crying. He swipes the mirror a second round and stares blankly into his own broken reflection.

Another faucet runs in the background. Breaker cups in his hands in the filled sink and splashes his face with water. With that, he turns and makes his way to the tub. It has filled and water begins to flood over the sides. He turns off the faucet. He's unhurried.

Before he steps into the tub, he crosses to the bathroom door and locks it. The moment he turns his back on the door, there is a knock.

"Son! Open this door! Son!" The knocking graduates to a pounding.

"Jonathan! It's your mother. We care about you and love you, honey. Please open the door!"

He ignores their pleas and calmly slides into the tub. Water flows over the sides, splashing to the floor.

"Jonathan! Son!" The violence of Jonathan's father ramming his shoulder into the door creates ripples on the bathwater. Jonathan has submerged his entire body except his head. He holds the razor that had been lying on the soap dish on the bathtub wall.

Both parents are screaming with hysteria, fear, and love as Jonathan slides the razor across the network of veins on his right wrist. The water quickly succumbs to the addition of blood and turns the color of a masterful watercolor sunset.

As he begins the same cut on the other wrist, the door smashes open, splinters flying in all directions. Jonathan's father grabs him under his arms and yanks him from the tub. He wraps a towel around the wound as blood flows freely.

"Call an emergency air-trans!" he screams to his wife as he holds his son and sobs.

"That was totally fucked up," Ranger says.

"You look like you've seen a ghost. I told you, Ranger. The Echo Dome can strip a man buck-naked right to his very soul. For some, it's just too much. Like looking in a mirror and not liking what they see."

"What I don't get is why they're so polite to each other when they're not fighting."

"Echo Dome combat is never personal, and there's no intent to damage the other guy. It's a war inside yourself. A battle of willpower and backbone, the point is keep your secrets from being told." Diamond pokes Ranger again. "A loss in the dome is less a win for your opponent than a failure you can only blame yourself for."

Ranger wipes sweat from his brow. "I can only imagine the crazy shit this guy One Shot has done." He pivots to the cage. "Let's go, Breaker! Let's get inside this asshole's head."

"Breaker! Your echo is public. Do you wish to concede?" asks Mr. Show. His panache from earlier has waned a bit.

Breaker is visibly shaken but says, "No. I do not."

"Very well. Jesus, begin at your discretion."

Jesus resumes the contest with his thunderous clap, and the combatants meet in the middle of the cage. They nod, then One Shot says, "Glad you made it. I need to get paid." Breaker nods again and sets to continue combat.

One Shot quickly closes again and throws a jab with his left followed by a right hook. Breaker dodges the jab and ducks the hook.

Breaker backs away a moment to recoup then immediately goes on the offensive. He throws a left-right jab combination, followed by roundhouse kick aimed at the hip sensor. His punches are easily dodged and he pulls his kick back before it has a chance to score. One Shot then steps into Breaker and shoves him to the cage floor.

"Stop!" cries Jesus. "Foul, One Shot. Physical contact. Echo deduction."

One Shot says, "Get up, bitch. I got places to be." Breaker rises from the floor. Anger and resentment bleed from the stare he gives his opponent.

"Begin!" says Jesus.

One Shot Charges toward Breaker with a vicious howl and swings wildly for his head. Breaker ducks the blow, and when One Shot turns around to face him, he leaps into the air, landing a front kick to the chest sensor within a sixteenth of an inch.

"Strike Recor…"

The jumbotron flickers. Sparks erupt from all four sides as the crowd gasps. The screen continues to flicker in and out of focus. Static plays four sides around.

"Um… Everyone remain calm," says Mr. Show with uncertainty. The static ends abruptly. A black screen and pure silence enslave the dome.

Silence…

The screens simultaneously flicker to life.

ECHO FORTHCOMING: ONE SHOT
ECHO FORTHCOMING: ONE SHOT
ECHO FORTHCOMING: ONE SHOT

The darkness is replaced by a front door.

"No!" screams One Shot in panic. "No!"

A hand softly knocks on the door. Once, then again two more times. A few moments later, the door opens to reveal a woman sitting on a floral-patterned sofa. She's beautiful, but her beauty has been damaged by sadness. Her eyes are heavy and she looks tired.

"It's your house, Thomas. You don't have to knock," she says, her voice dripping with sarcasm.

"I know. It's just…the way we left things the last time we spoke, I didn't just want to barge in," the man says softly.

"I don't care what you do. I've told you. It's over. I want a divorce," she says.

"I know the last couple of years have been tough. But I love you, Samantha. I love you for better or for worse. That's what we agreed to the day we were married."

"Stop it, Thomas! Just stop. I'm not doing this dance with you again. I don't love you." She turns abruptly and walks back into the living room. *"I haven't loved you in a very long time. Maybe never. I don't care about you. I don't even remotely love you in any semblance of how you feel for me. I just don't."*

The man crosses the threshold and passes the entry table where he carelessly throws rain gear and gloves upon it. He sees himself briefly in the mirror which hangs over the table. Thomas is One Shot.

"Sam, when we met all those years ago, you were broken. So was I. We swore we'd never feel that way again. Deceived by love. Affairs of the heart would never hurt us again. All those times you thanked me, hugged me, cried with me, made love to me—what? It was a lie? I don't believe it!"

"I don't know what you want me to say, Thomas. I don't want to be with you. I don't want to be around you. The thought of being intimate with you makes me want to vomit."

"My God, Sam. We have a daughter. What are we supposed to tell her?"

"Tell her what you want. I'm walking out that door and neither of you will ever see me again. And frankly, I don't give a shit!"

She walks briskly past One Shot and out the door, not even bothering to close it.

One Shot drops to his knees, crying. A moment later, he loses all control. Sliding completely to floor, he gives in to uncontrollable sobs, the song of the brokenhearted.

"One Shot, your echo is… oh dear"

One Shot lies on the floor of the cage in a near catatonic state. He is shaking. Rocking back and forth, he repeats. "Yes, I concede. Yes, I concede. Yes, I concede…"

"Son of a bitch!" roars Diamond.

"What?" says Ranger. "Are you kidding! That was amazing. This… is amazing!"

"Fucks me every time."

"What does?"

Diamond rips his bet ticket to shreds and throws it to the ground. "Love. It's the one wild card you can't ever predict."

"Love?"

"Love. Now let's get the fuck outa here and go see Hanson and that shitload of currency for all of us."

The two men flip up their rain gear, put on goggles, dig their hands into their pockets, and walk out into the neon rain.

Peach of a Delivery, That!
S. Elliot Brandis

IT'S THIRTY FUCKEN SEVEN DEGREES CELCIUS, yet here I am sitting in the sun watching my team play cricket. I'm slumped in an old camping chair threatening to fall apart at any moment, sipping from a bottle filled with piss-weak green cordial. The sizzle of my skin tells me that my sunblock is already failing. In other words, it's a normal summer's day in rural Australia.

"Howzitgaan, mate?" Johnno asks, flopping down on the grass beside me.

"Nah, yeah, not bad. The usge."

"Ya fucken sure? You look like a redback just crawled up your arse."

"Honestly, mate? Cunt's fucked."

"Yeah?"

"Yeah."

Johnno looks out at the game. Baz the Big Unit, this huge prick from the next town down, is bowling. He's already knocked over two of our blokes—one bowled, the other caught behind—in two bloody overs. We're rubbish and all that, but even for us this is a shithouse start.

"Anything ya wanna talk about?" Johnno asks with an intonation that tells me he really hopes there isn't.

"Nah'm good mate"

"Fair enough." The wrinkles around his eyes drop away, a sign of relief.

Y'see, in the bush, well... Blokes don't talk about feelings and shit. It's all a bit much, right? The correct answer to *How's the missus?*, *How's work?*, and *Howzitgaan?* is invariably, *Not bad.* Even if things are bad. Hell, *especially* if things are bad.

A shout of *Howzat!?* rings out across the field. Baz is flapping his arms around like an epileptic ibis. The umpire considers his appeal for a moment, nods, then raises his index finger. Our third wicket has fallen. Which means that it's my turn to bat. Fucken great.

I hoick myself up, grab my bat and gloves, and begin the slow walk out to the pitch.

"What's the score?" I call out to the scorekeeper's table.

"Three-for-twelve," the old biddies reply in unison, a touch too perky. "No pressure."

"Righto."

But the thing is, I'm not feeling that much pressure to begin with. The game's fucked, sure, but I've got other things on my mind. Like the other night.

There's not really a glamourous way to frame this, but I was sitting on the dunny when it happened. Literally an outdoor shithouse, made of warping timber and crooked sheets of corrugated iron. Even with an evening breeze cutting through the gaps, it clung on to the day's heat. My skin was crusted with salt.

As tends to happen in the middle of woop woop, my phone lost reception. That's how I knew my shit had concluded. I rested my phone on the concrete-slab floor, beside my sweating tin of beer, and reached for the toilet paper. I wiped, dropped, and… *ah fuck*, it didn't drop. The shit-stained wad stuck to my fingers like a dirty koala joey clinging to its mum. It held on for dear life.

I tried to peel it away, but the bastard was fixed fast. I grabbed more paper with my opposite hand and did my best to clean myself up. Thankfully, those latter wads dropped into the abyss below. I yanked up my shorts, toddled out of the box like a drunk penguin, and ran my problem hand under the tap. The paper broke away as the water soggied it up. It wasn't a pretty sight, though, I can tell you that. I'll spare you the shitty details.

That's when I noticed that my fingers were pink.

I dug into my pocket, grabbed my phone, and flicked on the torch. It near blinded me in the dim evening. Even the moon can't be arsed some nights. My hand was shaking, making the shadows frolic.

Not only were my fingers a sickly sorta pink, but I swear to Christ they had little fucken hooks. Every digit except my thumb looked like the surface of a cat's tongue. Slightly coarser, even. It was no bloody wonder the paper had stuck. My hand was deadset munted.

So I did what any responsible adult would do. I went to my room, had a cold shower, and drunk myself to sleep. I woke up in my grundies, sweating like a paedo in a playground. Thankfully, my fingers had returned to normal. I hadn't the foggiest what had happened.

Which brings us to now—me trudging out onto a cricket field.

Now let me tell you this: there isn't a more beautiful place in the world than a cricket oval in summer. The grass is trimmed short so that it near about sparkles. In the middle, the pitch shimmers, the sun beating down on it like an alcoholic father. Twenty-two yards of dead turf crushed to buggery by a roller. And when you reach the middle, you're the man. The field drops away around you, like you're on the world's least elevated stage. You're a knight with two missions: score some runs and, for fuck's sake, don't lose your bloody wicket.

"Bit early to be seeing you here, Ned," says Dicky, their little turd of a wicket-keeper. He grins at me with his ruddy wombat face.

"Yeah, steady on."

They call me Ned because of Ned Kelly, an infamous Australian bushranger. Now, I don't reckon I look naught like the fucken bloke, but I've got a big-arse beard and thousand-mile stare when I'm agro. Sometimes that's all it takes. Dicky, on the other hand, is named after Dicky Knee—this weird little puppet on a stick from an old variety show, *Hey Hey It's Saturday!* He doesn't look shit like his namesake either, but they have a similar affinity for being lippy little smartarses.

"Learned how to bat yet?"

"Last night, mate."

He cackles.

Now, listen here, sledging is an integral part of the game of cricket. This little dickweed is going to be in my ear for ages, so long as I can last that long. So it's never a proper convo. Just nips here and there. Niggles. Little barbs to shit me off and wear me down.

I ask the umpire for the line of my centre stump, then dutifully mark the pitch with my boot. I check my pad straps, give my box a knock, and do a quick once-around to survey the field. They don't think much of me. The field is up close, ready to pounce. Which is fair enough, given the bastard of a season I've been having.

"Right arm over," the umpire calls.

I offer him a nod and settle into my stance. I knock the pitch a couple of times with my bat for good measure. Three for twelve. Here we go.

The bowler prances up, swinging his arms about like a full-blown wanker. Sometimes fellas see something cool on telly and work it into their action. But even then, this is a sight. He looks like a frog in a blender. It's his first delivery of the game, Baz having finished his over the previous ball, so I dunno what to expect. Never faced this bloke in my life.

He jumps in tight to the stumps and flicks one down.

I take a stride forward and block it.

Yeah, cricket is about patience. But I've already learned two things: he fancies himself as an off-spin bowler, but the pitch isn't offering much turn yet. I reckon he might toss up a couple, to draw me into doing something stupid, then try firing in a few darts. Maybe an arm ball, if he's got a decent one. We'll see.

I walk out and tap the centre of the pitch. There's no real point in doing this, but it's an excuse to chat to the batsman up the other end. It's my ol' mate, Bondi. So called because he used to live near Bondi Beach and pretty much won't shut up about the place. He's a teacher at the local school. Decent enough bloke but with that douchey Sydney shtick boiling water couldn't wash off.

"What d'ya reckon?" I ask.

"Not much action out there. Baz is swinging it, though. So we might want go after this new guy."

"Go the tonk?"

"Work it around a bit. We can't risk another wicket.

"Yeah, fair call."

I wander back to my crease. The bowler is already back at his mark, shining the ball on his trousers. He's eyeing me off for breaking his rhythm. That's the other reason to have a chat—throw 'em off their game a bit.

He hurls down the next delivery and, sure enough, I was right. He's given it air, looping it up above my eye line. Fuck patience—he's over pitched it. I stride forward, load up my swing, and put my back into it.

Thwack.

There it is. The sound of leather on willow. That heavenly crunch.

The ball fizzles over the infield, heading at speed to cow corner. It reaches the boundary on one hop. Four runs. Easy as you like.

Bondi glances down the pitch at me, brow furrowed. I respond with a shrug. Like, what the fuck do you expect me to do, mate? That was an absolute gift. Nothing to knot your knickers over.

"Well, bugger me up the arse," Dicky quips.

"Bit early for that, mate."

"Just shocked, is all. Haven't seen you hit one like that for yonks."

"I told you, I learned last night."

The bowler starts his run up. Off-spinners love to rush through their overs. So I shimmy into place, rocking my bat up behind me.

"Do it again, then," Dicky says under his breath as he crouches down.

Bog standard chat, here. It's a lot easier to get out swinging than it is playing sensibly. Still, I wouldn't mind having a crack. Gotta teach the new fella how we do it out here, yeah?

Froggy flights it up again, this time a little outside off. I step towards the pitch of the ball and crunch it on the half volley. I can feel in my bones that I've middled it. The ball sails through the covers, skipping along the turf.

I dash out of my crease, starting a run. But the outfield is quick today. I slow to a trot as I watch the ball bobble over the boundary rope. Another four. I bump my glove against Bondi's. He can't give me shit for that one. It was fucken textbook, safe as houses.

"So what the fuck d'ya do last night, Ned?" Dicky asks as I return to my crease. "Tug yourself with a new lube?"

My smile drops away. *Last night.* What the fuck was that, anyway? I feel a touch queasy thinking about it.

Velcro crackles as I undo my glove, giving my offending hand another look. It's normal enough—a little splotchy maybe? I don't wanna see a doc. Haven't seen one since I was a sprog. Sure as hell don't wanna start now.

"You right, mate?"

"Yeah."

"You look like you found out the postie rooted your mum."

"Probably did, mate. Never knew my Dad."

"Shit, aye. Nothing personal."

"All good. Just feeling off today."

"You get bit or something, mate?"

"Maybe."

I barely have time to put my glove back on when the offie prick is half way down the track. He bowls it a little quicker, finally finding a good length. I play a defensive shot, not quite feeling another big whack. The ball dribbles back down the pitch.

"You ever watched Spiderman?" I ask Dicky.

"Was on telly last week."

"You reckon that could happen? Get bit by some radioactive redback and have weird shit happen?"

"Steady on, princess. You've got eight runs. Not exactly in superhero territory yet."

I look around at the field. A couple of blokes are shifting around, like they've already got a plan for me. Like hell they do.

"Yeah, nah, not like that. Something happened, is all."

"If you reckon you can bat now, then I'll have to bloody agree with ya."

I retake my stance. Again, the ball is bang on a length. I offer a half-hearted prod, not knowing what else to do with it. As fate would have it, the ball nips away sharply off the seam. An arm ball, maybe. It sure as hell didn't look like one. It nicks the edge of my bat and it sails into the waiting gloves of Dicky.

The mongrel bowler celebrates like he bowled Graham Gooch around the legs. He drops to his knees and pumps his fists like a knob. The cunt wants to be noticed, that's for sure. Behind me, Dicky is yippin' like a bunyip. I don't even turn to look. I'm out, caught behind.

"Bad luck, Spidey," he calls out.

"Get fucked," I reply.

I tuck my bat under my arm and begin my walk of shame. Behind me, I know Bondi's fuming. He can get fucked, too. That ball came out of nowhere.

The rest of the inning goes by pretty quick. I zone out like I'm two beers past drunk, engulfed in myself. It's a mixture of rage and worry. Rage because I completely screwed up, dug our hole a little deeper, and worry because—well you know. I'm a freak. Worse, I still can't bat.

Thankfully, the team recovers a little. Mostly because of Bondi, who scores a well-paced half century. At the end of our forty overs, we've set a total of 180. Which isn't good, but it's decent enough after the four for twenty mess I left us in. Something tells me I'm gonna be hearing of Bondi's efforts for a while. From the man himself, no doubt. Sydney pricks—I told you.

When we take the ground, I'm sent out to field at deep fine leg. You see this a lot in park cricket. I'm essentially a mop-up man, for when the batsman gets a bit streaky with an edge, or the wicketkeeper fucks up, or the bowler gets a bit wild. All three will happen in a few overs, believe me. We're not exactly The Invincibles.

For the rest of the time, it means I'm standing out in no man's land alone with my thoughts. Not exactly what I want right now. But I drag myself through several overs, not doing anything worth mentioning.

Eventually, some fat fucker skies a top edge. It rockets into the pale sky, right into the goddamn sun. These bastards are the hardest to catch—they should be easy, but the sun is extra bitey this time of the day. I squint as I position myself, trying to read the arc of the ball. It twirls around like a bat with one wing. At the last minute, I realised I've misjudged it. I swear the thing jags in mid-air. But I stick out my right arm and contort my body. Somehow, the ball sticks between my forefinger and thumb.

It's a goddamn Christmas miracle.

My team mates flock over to me like seagulls chasing a chip. They scruff my hair and pat my bum. Some grub sticks his tongue in my ear.

"You're a lucky cunt," Bondi says.

"It's the lucky country, aye?"

"Want to bowl next over? Ride the rainbow?"

My eyebrows spring up. I don't get called on to bowl much, especially this early in the inning. But hey—I messed up with the willow, so I might as well have a crack.

"Sure thing," I say.

So there I am a couple of balls later, getting ready to bowl. Here's another reason I hate that fancy fuckwit that got me out—I'm an off-spinner too. Not a very good one, mind. But the pitches in our comp don't offer shit for spinners. That's my excuse, at least. And that's why it hurts to get out to one of my own kind. *Especially* to a gem like that.

"How's the field?" Bondi calls out.

I shrug. "Yeah, all right."

"Rip it, Ned."

"Righto."

I mosey on up to the popping crease. Unlike that froggy bloke, my action is no-frills. I run up head on and keep the fuss to a minimum. It's about momentum, not theatrics. Hit the pitch hard, square my shoulder, and try to keep the revs up.

There's two moments in cricket that I'd describe as orgasmic. One is when you slog the ball right outta the middle of the bat, the sweet spot. You can feel the wood ping like a spring. It's effortless. The other, as a spinner, is when the ball comes out of the hand *just* right. You can feel your index finger grip the seam as you roll your fingers across it, sending the ball spiralling out on the perfect axis. In the air, you can barely even see the spin. The stiches line up perfectly. Until it lands, that is. Then... *zing!* It tears into the turf like it has teeth, bouncing up with bite and angling in to the batsman's guts.

Even better—when you're in the zone, I swear you can see the exact moment the batsman realises he's fucked. His bat is already stabbing out, his footwork confused. But he doesn't have time to adjust to the deviation of the ball. He's off balance. Up shit creek.

And that's when I hear the death rattle.

Somehow I've pitched the ball outside off and taken out his leg stump. The bails fly into the air, announcing his departure. A couple of moments later, I'm mobbed again. I've taken a wicket with my first ball. I am, for a brief moment, no longer that dickhead that threw away his wicket.

"Peach of a delivery, that," Lefty, our lazy-eyed wicketkeeper, says.

"Just about turned square," agrees Bondi, who was fielding in the slips.

"Luck," I say. "Mighta hit a pebble."

"Well, that's two flukes today. Get lucky again and it might as well be a trend."

I shake my hand as I return to my mark. My finger is stinging. From that streaky catch, I reckon. I glance down at my hand, hoping to hell that it isn't swelling. Instead, I'm greeted by the last thing I wanna see—my fingers are pink, those little hooks standing proud.

My vision goes wavy. I rattle my noggin, doing my best not to faint. There's something very wrong with me. Yet... well I'll be fucked if it isn't helping. No wonder the ball turned so much. My messed up skin is literally gripping the seam as though it's Velcro. I'm in perhaps the only situation where such a condition would actually help.

Maybe I *am* lucky. In my own boofhead way.

"Knock him over!" Lefty calls.

I take a deep breath, try to focus.

Worry about it tonight, after a few beers. I've never taken more than two wickets before. If I'm ever gonna have a shot, it's right now. I stare down the new batsman and start my approach.

Blocked.

Then again.

In all, he defends four balls straight, not taking a single risk. The ball is absolutely zipping off the wicket. It darts around like a horny rat. By now, my confidence is peaking.

Bondi jogs up to me. "Throw him a tempter," he says. "Draw him out of his shell."

"Sure thing, Skip."

...probably work it down leg.

"Down leg? You're off your tits," I say.

Bondi cocks his head. "Uh, what?"

Yeah, that's it. Fuck being on strike to this bastard.

I glance at the batsmen, but they're nowhere near each other. But, sure enough, the bloke on strike is looking down his leg side, where the fielder has strayed a little too deep. A smart batsman could work the ball across his body, taking off the pace and allowing an easy single.

Bugger me.

I can read his mind.

My heart jumps up in my chest, thrashing about like I've just finished a dash. Hook hands. Mind reading. Exactly what in the fuck is happening to me?

Fucken weird cunt, this one.

Righto, that's it. This arse-wipe is getting out. Next ball.

Nobody insults a bloody cricketing superhero.

An idea strokes. I should bowl a doosra. A doosra is... well, it's a delivery that spins the other way. Instead of turning into the batman's body, it'll nip back the opposite. Which is a great bloody idea, but it's next to near impossible to bowl one without bending your elbow. And getting no-balled for chucking is a good way to mess up your season. Nobody likes a chucker. Especially not the old blokes that hand out suspensions.

But...

I have a feeling I can pull it off. With my hook fingers, that is. I don't *need* to bend my elbow. If I can grip onto the seam with my skin, as unnatural as that is, I reckon I can impart enough spin using only my wrist. It's fluky, of course. I mean, clearly. We're dealing with something that's never been done. But if this dickstain is gonna play across his body, then a ball spinning away is the perfect delivery. I'll either trap him leg before, knock over his castle, or draw an edge. Either way, the cunt's fucked.

The umpire turns around. "Today, maybe?"

"Sorry."

I stride in with confidence, clutching onto the ball for dear life. I'm basically fucking with the physics of the game. If I can pull this off, I'm a wizard. The sultan of spin.

My front foot lands. My arm comes over. I roll my fingers over the ball as per my usual action, except—for a split second—I don't let go. My hooks grip the seam as I splay out my fingers, reversing the direction of the spin.

And, like that, my plan works. The batsman is completely bamboozled. The ball zips up the opposite way, bouncing like it's hit a landmine. It somehow clips the handle of his bat and bobbles through the keeper. Lefty's eyes light up as he cradles it. He's never seen such a thing. Certainly not in park cricket.

I'm swarmed *again*. In a few short balls, I've gone from a middle-order batsman that royally duffed it to a spin bowling maestro. With one ball remaining in the tenth over, we've got them three for forty. Our fortunes have done a one-eighty. And I am the catalyst. The spark.

Now, I won't bother you with the rest of the inning. I'm sure I sound like a cocky cunt already. But, long story short, we bowl 'em out for 90, half of the total we set.

And my figures are unheard of. Seven wickets for eleven runs. In short, it's a club record. But that's pretty easy to do when you can read minds and bowl hand grenades. I'm surprised they even scored eleven off me.

After the match, we hit the clubhouse. It's an old wooden building as old as time, but beers are cheap and plentiful. In local cricket like this, the after-game sesh is as much a feature as the game itself. The opposition suddenly become your mates and, if you're lucky, the umpires too. Most of them are old fellas with stories longer than the Murray-Darling. Two drinks in and the sound of laughter fills the dusty air.

There's a hand on my shoulder. "Let me buy you a beer."

I crane my neck around. It's the fancy prick that got me out. But it's all good. I returned the favour and won us the game to boot.

"Ain't gonna say no," I say with a grin.

He fetches us a couple of stubbies and before long, we're having a yarn.

"You new here, then?" I ask.

"Moved in last week."

I ponder this fact for a moment. I love this shithole, don't get me wrong, but it's rare that new folks come to the region. Good luck finding a job. Since the mines started shutting down, the economy in the bush is basically fucked.

"Family here?" I ask.

"Work."

"Yeah? Where at."

He considers my question for a moment, rubbing his head with a sweaty hand.

"Government," he says at last.

"Come to fuck us a little more?"

"Hey, at least I bought you a drink first."

He forces a laugh, but I don't give one back. I'm genuinely curious as to what he's doing in these parts. I let the silence linger, hoping that he'll fill it with more than a joke. He looks me dead in the eye.

You know why I'm here, he thinks, projecting it right into my goddamn skull.

Mate, I can assure you I don't know shit.

Do you know Sandra Ryan?

Well, yeah. She's my mum. Dead now, mind you.

But she never told you? About your… heritage.

Told me what?

By now, we look like a right pair of creeps. Staring at each other in silence, somehow talking in our heads. I break the tension by skulling my beer. I down it in a few long gulps, letting it chill my now churning guts. He waits 'til I slam down my empty.

Ned…

Yeah?

You're not from this place.

I can assure you I fucken well am.

He throws back his drink, finishing it as fast as I did mine. I swear even he's a little nervous now. His eyes are near glowing, his stare intense. The air around us grows thick and heavy.

You're not from this planet. You're one of us.

Us?

And I'm here to unlock your potential.

Veloxity
Daniel Arthur Smith

PASCAL LAY BOUND BENEATH a broken ceiling fan. Strapped tight to a table, he'd spent the last hour or so watching the unbalanced propeller blades slowly spin with a rhythmic *creak-lisp*, *creak-lisp*, *creak-lisp*. The ceiling above the rotating blades was yellowed and dingy, the tin tiles coated with a patina so thick that a hardened honey resin oozed from their seams and down the side of the fan's mount. He calculated that it must've taken decades to build up. Even the dust-laden strands of the long-abandoned corner cobweb dripped tan. Wherever he was, the place was a dump.

The hypnotic spin of the fan was interrupted by voices outside of the room—two men—one was too soft for Pascal to make out, but the other's words, deep and gruff, were easily decipherable. "Remember," said the man. "This has to happen fast. If the kid misses the race, you don' get paid."

Pascal recognized the voice. It was Abner, a mob fixer from the racing pits.

Pascal attempted to hurl himself to the side, shift his weight, to break free from the table. No doing. The straps were firm. He was too tightly bound.

The door squealed open. "An' 'ere he is. Tha League's finest pilot—Pascal Razore."

Abner bent over the table. A gold-toothed smile spread wide across the gangster's meaty face as he gave Pascal a pat on the cheek. "How ya doin', Pascal my boy?"

Pascal bit into the tight gag that muzzled his mouth and raged out a defiant gurgle from the back of his throat.

"Ha, ha. That's the fire we're payin' for."

A second head appeared across the table from Abner, this one wearing a surgical cap and mask.

"Pascal, I want you to meet Doctor—"

"Ha hum," interrupted the masked man.

Abner's eyes rolled up to face the man. "Rat," he said. "Anonymity." He set his attention back down to Pascal. "He's the one who'll be givin' you your upgrade."

"Hello, Mister Razore," said the masked man. "How are you doing today?" He paused for Pascal to issue a muffled response then continued. "I see," he said. "Don't worry. This is simply a preliminary exam. You'll be moved to a proper sanitary space for the procedure."

Abner chuckled and said, "Wouldn' be in ma interest, were you to come ta any 'arm."

Pascal's head thrashed side to side as he fought the restraints. Guttural howls escaped through the gag as well as spouts of spittle.

Abner's face drew closer as he pressed his hands into Pascal's shoulder. "Relax," he said. Unable to turn away, Pascal's face contorted at the dose of rotten breath. "It just makes practical sense," Abner continued. "We're doing you a favor. Every pilot at this level of the league has already replaced their limbs— that is, every pilot but you. And a good many have swapped out their hearts and lungs for *beaters*. Doc, help me out here."

The masked man lifted a large black plastic hypo syringe into Pascal's view, loaded a cartridge into the end, and twisted it until it let out a loud hiss. Captive or not, Pascal resolved that he wasn't going to make it easy for them. He flailed as hard as he could, but it was pointless. Abner's weight held him firm. "Stay still, boy. Remember, we have Dalia."

With that, Pascal settled. He did remember. They had his sister, which meant they had him. He locked eyes with the gangster. It was coming back to him. Pascal nodded, and let his body go limp.

Abner backed away and the Doctor who chose no name shot the hypo into the side of Pascal's neck.

A soft velvet blanket of blackness surrounded Pascal. In the distance, a finite point of white light, a beacon, grows ever brighter, ever closer. The edges of the light shimmer, blead into the black, then in an abrupt thrust of acceleration, the white envelopes him with a wave of warmth and euphoria.

His scalp pulls tight and his fingers and toes clench. Helmet, gloves, boots. The roar of his veloxity racer fills the white. Then, in an instantaneous flash, the white dissipates. He is in the cockpit of his veloxity racer, in the wake of another driver, climbing the ninety-degree incline of the Nürburgring corkscrew. With little effort, he hangs tight to the edge of the forged-steel track, using the g-forces to propel his racer forward through loop one, two, three, then onto the ramp where he punches his kinetic energy reserve, gracefully sling-shotting his veloxity up and over his forward opponent and across the thirty-meter jump.

Despite the maneuver, he lands smoothly—nine-thousand kilometers from the Nordic Meg's Nürburgring complex—onto the chromium track of the New Macau Colossal raceway. A thousand streaks of neon—green, pink, orange, and red—stream overhead as he glides high speed through the raceway's famed Tunnel of Light. To his left, another veloxity racer is rapidly moving in. Pascal doesn't need the bump. He activates reverse thrusters, slides behind the racer, then uses his opponent's draft to overtake him inside the next turn. The other racer attempts to do the same to Pascal on the turn after that, the hairpin descending switchback, but overcompensates his tail-toss, careens into the wall, and explodes on contact. Pascal breaks from the tunnel to pounding rain—and yet another track. Storm-blackened clouds loom low over a long, wide, straightaway. Pascal recognizes the gradually-descending strip of suspension bridge and the towering cyclone track on the horizon. He has five kilometers to reach the speed necessary to ascend the WestPac Death Spiral. As he accelerates, the black carbon cables suspending the dark resin track phase into a constant of grey and the veloxity racers surrounding him begin to blur. At max speed, he hits the cyclone. Pascal is one with his machine, breathing with it, the veloxity engine the beat of his heart. Bright orange blasts flash around him as other racers—failing to hold their lines—collide with the rails and each other.

Pascal's in the winner's circle. His sister Dalia steps from backstage holding a huge bouquet of red roses. She reaches out to hug him, but before he can embrace her, she is pulled away by two indigo suited men, one at each arm. "Help me," she mouths, as they drag her across the platform.

But Pascal cannot move.

Behind Dalia, from the backstage shadows, steps Abner, the gold tooth gleaming from his smile.

Pascal screams silent, and in his scream, he is enveloped by the white then, as rapidly, by the blackness. There is nothing. Then the slow rhythmic *creak-lisp*, *creak-lisp*, *creak-lisp*.

Pascal awoke with a gasp. He was still in the room, but something had changed. Both the propeller fan and Abner hovered above. Instinctively, he stretched his jaw wide, then realized the gag had been removed. He shifted his arms. The straps were gone as well.

Pascal met eyes with Abner, then lunged upward to seize him.

He only made it inches from the table then crashed back down.

Abner let out a mocking laugh. "*Ha, ha, ha.*" Then, as confident as Pascal had ever heard him, said, "It's the anesthesia. The reason you can't move. That's why there's no straps." Abner threw his hands up and added, "No need."

Pascal lashed out, but found he was only able to hiss out the words, "You son of a—" Again, he tried to speak, but could not.

"No need for the gag either," said Abner.

Pascal made up for the loss of speech with flaring nostrils and a burning stare. He willed Abner's throat crushed, visualized the gangster clawing at his neck as his face shot first to red then blue.

But as powerful as Pascal's will was, Abner remained unaffected.

"Relax, my boy," said Abner. "You'll need your strength soon enough."

Pascal's eyes followed Abner as he walked toward the far end of the table. Abner stopped in front of a machine with a screen displaying fluid colors melding into each other. "I can't read this," he said. "But the Doctor tells me that this somehow monitors that neural lace wetware you have 'neath your skull cap." Abner placed his finger on the screen and allowed it to follow a string of blue bubbling through a puddle of red. "He put a *beater* in you. When you're plugged into your veloxity, your rig will take care of your blood and breathing. That'll free up processing in your lacework."

Pascal attempted to shake his head. The movement was subtle but enough for Abner to notice. "Look," said Abner. "You know better than anyone that this is a sport where a fraction of a second can make a difference. The Cardia..." He looked across the room.

From beyond Pascal's peripheral, the doctor said, "The Cardiac Control Center."

Abner nodded. "Yeah. In race conditions, this Cardiac Control Center takes up a good deal of your anatomic capacity. It's the most we could squeeze out without removing your gear shift." Abner twirled his finger at Pascal's crotch. "We're not monsters, after all."

Pascal understood what Abner was saying. The neural lace implant was the interface pilots used to control the veloxity racers with maximum efficiency. What Abner called a *beater* was a prosthetic circulatory system that would jack directly into veloxity racer, minimizing his brains resource utilization, freeing up valuable functions to focus on the race.

Abner came back to the head of the table. "Look, boy, you should be thanking me. We had you run simulation while you were under, and let me be the first to tell you, you're about to be the fastest pilot the league's ever seen. The only way you'd be faster is if you used that neural lace of yours to transfer your conscience directly into a synth automated vehicle. And that's just not allowed for the big money."

Pascal mouthed a word that Abner understood. "No."

Abner shook his head. "Now you listen and listen good. As far as your sister knows, she's on a complimentary spa weekend up until the race. She's fine, and you'll see her again. All you have to do is win the race."

"Hello, Race Day fans! I'm Denny Coulier and here with me is Ryan Hunter and were coming to you from New Macau, the shining gem of the WestPac and home of the Colossus, the Homeland Racing League's newly-designed velocity track where pilots from across the system have gathered for this pinnacle racing event."

"That's right, Denny. The best pilots in the league have gathered here for what we've been told will be a race like no other, and that's largely due to the vastness of the newly-completed Colossus raceway. This track is unbelievable, consisting of multiple loops, curves, a corkscrew spiral, and, unique to this track, the Tunnel of Light—a labyrinth, consisting of five short, rapid switchback curves that start with a descending hairpin. High speeds make it one of the league's most dangerous runs."

"Ryan, why don't we just call it what it is—deadly. One malfunction or wrong decision on the Colossal could mean grave consequences. This is no off-world race where drivers transfer into a synthetic rig. There are no syns allowed in the Homeland and that includes syn veloxities."

"That's right. But that's not the only reason—the league requires mortal pilots because they want drivers. Let's take a look at the big screen and into the cockpit of fan favorite and virtuoso display of talent—Driver 23, Pascal Razore."

"Pascal has yet to drop his visor, giving us the rare glimpse of those glowing, fire blue eyes."

"That's due to his neural lacework. When he's on the track, he'll be executing multiple velocity interfaces per psycho-second."

"And for this race, he'll be firing that interface faster than ever. As you know, Pascal just had his heart and lungs removed and replaced with a prosthetic Cardiac Control Center. Rumor is that he had the upgrade procedure done to free up some anatomic processing."

"Imagine the commitment. Removing your organs for a race advantage."

"You don't climb in to be a driver. You do it because you're driven."

From the instant Pascal jacked into his veloxity, the dead piece of metal became a living breathing extension of himself.

He'd kept the advantage discrete—as discrete as a top racer could get away with.

By design, Pascal qualified to a mid-grid position start and, with a pace averaging six-hundred and fifty kilometers per hour, had kept that place in the pack for the duration of the race.

In the final lap, an image of Dalia flashed on the augment of his windscreen, a reminder from his sponsor that it was time to stop steering and start driving.

"For you," Pascal whispered. Then, as if easing his head back into a pillow, he transcended to slipstream.

The Tunnel of Light became a kaleidoscope of neon and black, and before him lit a glowing path—the slipstream mapping his way forward. It was now that he could fully exercise the power of his neural lace, calibrating gear shift and acceleration against the force and angle of the steel forged track. Through his mental interface, he flipped open the top flap of the rear wing to reduce drag in the straight away. The veloxity's straight-line speed increased. Pascal held the throttle as he rapidly closed in on the veloxity, a blue blur in front of him, then—just as he had done in the simulation—he froze the front end and tail-tossed the rear of his racer around the point of the hairpin, easily sliding sideways past his opponent and into an unprecedented one-eighty spin from the back, propelling his veloxity down to the labyrinth's next switchback. With an effortless rhythm, he repeated the tail-toss maneuver five more times, climbing high to the side of the last curve to gain momentum for the first loop. He ascended the ramp without need of a kinetic punch, instead relying on the wake of the next emerald veloxity ahead to reduce drag. At the top of the loop, his peripheral caught the colored blurs streaming below—the orange and purple veloxity racers flying from the Cyclone exit ramp through the center of the loop. They were far behind. He exited the loop almost touching the forward racer. The next hairpin was right ahead and he planned another tail-toss pass, but his opponent tail-tossed inside first. Pascal could only mimic then follow. He planned to make up for it on the next curve, the first

Dog Bowl, but the emerald velocity went in tight to the inside—too tight. Pascal kept a line around the bowl while his opponent tail-tossed himself to an out of control spin out. Pascal didn't look back; he held the edge of the track out of the Dog Bowl up into the wide parabolic curve. He let his eye drift to the track augment before him and the half dozen microdot blips representing the remaining racers. He was in second. All but one of the trailing racers were far behind, but the lead was close. He raised his eyes to a ruby blur rounding the second loop of the corkscrew spiral to his front.

Pascal dropped down into the first loop and held his line through the corkscrew and onto the track's second wide parabolic bend. His velocity soared vertically as he rounded the curve's highest point. Though he couldn't turn his head to the side to see, the dash augment told him the red velocity was already rounding the second loop of the Cyclone spiral below. For the entirety of the race, Pascal had taken the Cyclone the same way, coming in high on the turn to build up speed then burrowing into the looping curves down to the ramp a hundred meters below. Like most every element of the Colossal, a racer needed the speed to keep from falling. It would never occur to a pilot to slow or stop; that could mean suicide. But in that instant, it occurred to Pascal. Perhaps it was the connection to his racer that gave him the confidence, or maybe just that he was truly the best pilot the league had ever seen.

In a flash decision, Pascal froze the right front tire, propelling the tail of his velocity up in a straight vertical, his nose pointed down the center of the Cyclone. His velocity hung above then slid down the inert parabolic curve and into the Cyclone.

Pascal, so deep in the moment, so tied to his racer, transcended the raceway.

It had never been done.

Never imagined.

A hundred thousand lights flashed as the fans surrounding the raceway frantically raised their vids to catch Pascal's free fall from up high down the Cyclone spiral.

Meters from the bottom, Pascal flipped the fins, lifting the nose enough to meet the angle of the exit loop. Then, just before touching down, he punched both the thrusters and the kinetic energy release.

His veloxity kissed the track, launched up off the ramp, and through the center of the giant loop.

If Pascal could have heard the crowd—at the raceway and those glued to vids across the systems—he would have heard an immense silence followed by an eruption of applause as each and every spectator howled out a victory call.

Pascal landed the thirty-meter jump far in the lead. The ruby veloxity would never come close to catching up. The kinetic energy reserve faded fast but not before pushing him past the third wide parabolic bend and into the final straight at track record speeds. To Pascal, the track had become a glowing path; to the spectators, he was a ghost. He blew through the second Dog Bowl and the final parabolic curve. Pascal caught the winning checkered flag racing at seven-hundred kilometers an hour.

He dropped into the cooling lane then circled to the winner's circle where his crew waited. He slammed his hands against his dash, a signal for his team to release the cage that bolted him in. As the hydraulics whirred, he frantically searched the faces of the crowd for his sister.

The cage popped and Pascal attempted to lift himself only to remember he was cabled to his velocity. Again, he slammed his hands onto his dash. Two of his pit crew lifted him from his rig, then pulled his helmet and his connection to the racer. His head went light and his chest tightened. Pascal threw his arms out to catch himself from falling. A member of his crew grabbed him from behind before he fell to the ground and another helped to prop Pascal up. Then, the blood that was absent rushed back in as neural lace regained control of his *beater*.

Roses landed at his feet. Photographers surrounded him. The league commissioner shoved a golden trophy in his hand and a magnum of champagne in the other. Pascal had won the race; the track record belonged to him. But his only concern was his sister. Dread filled him. Then, from the side of the crowd, one voice called out unique from the others. "Pascal," she said. "Pascal, you've won!"

There was Dalia with a smile on her face and a bouquet in one arm and Abner on the other. A hundred questions came from every direction as reporters jostled forward. Pascal handed the trophy to closest one. The reporter took it, startled. He handed the champagne to his crew chief and approached his sister.

He reached out his arms to her. "Are you all right?" he asked, scowling at the gold toothed gangster as he pushed himself between them.

Abner snickered and said, "I told you she'd be fine."

As Pascal embraced Dalia, she whispered in his ear. "I'm sorry," she said. "But this was the only way we could get you to do the upgrade. No one will ever beat you now."

ABOUT THE AUTHORS

Will Swardstrom is a speculative fiction author. His latest novel is *Blink*, the first adventure in *The Utility Company* series, co-written with his brother Paul. He also has two full length novels, *Dead Sleep* and *Dead Sight*, and is at work on the finale in the trilogy. He also has three stories in The Future Chronicles anthology series (*Uncle Allen* in *The Alien Chronicles, Z Ball* in *The Z Chronicles,* and *The Control* in *The Immortality Chronicles*). Each of those anthologies has charted in the Top 5 on the SF Anthology list and The Alien Chronicles reached as high as #6 on the Overall Top 100 List. The Control from The Immortality Chronicles has been nominated for Best American Science Fiction. He also has a few stories set in Hugh Howey's WOOL Universe among his various other short stories and novellas. He lives in Southern Illinois with his wife and two kids.

Nathan M. Beauchamp started writing stories at nine years old and never stopped. From his first grisly tales about carnivorous catfish, mole detectives, and cyborg housecats, his interests have always delved into strange waters. Nathan works in finance so that he can support his habit of putting words together in the hope that someone will read them. His hobbies include reading, photography, arguing for sport, and pondering the eventual heat death of the universe. He has published many short stories in magazines and anthologies, and holds an MFA in creative writing from Western State. He lives in Colorado with his wife and two young boys. Nathan co-created the award winning YA science fiction series *Universe Eventual* where he writes as N.J. Tanger. The series includes *Chimera*, *Helios*, and *Ceres* and the prequel *Ascension*.

For more information, visit ntanger.com

Bob Williams currently lives in Nashville, Tennessee after stops in Mississippi, Louisiana, Ohio, and Washington. He lives with his beautiful 6 year old daughter Kate, dogs Hank Henry, and two cats Cassidy and Wally. Bob sincerely hopes you enjoy reading his words as much as he enjoys writing them.

S. Elliot Brandis is an engineer and author from Brisbane, Australia. He writes post-apocalyptic and dystopian fiction, often infused with a variety of outside elements. He is a lover of beer, baseball, and science fiction.

His novels are about outlaws, outcasts, and outsiders.

For more information, visit selliotbrandis.com

Jessica West (a.k.a. West1Jess) is currently pursuing a state of self-induced psychosis, also known as writing. In the past, she has worked for Wal-Mart, a lawyer, and a bank. Now if she could just get a couple years experience with the IRS and the NSA, world domination is in the bag.
Jess lives in Acadiana with three daughters still young enough to think she's cool and a husband who knows better but likes her anyway.

For more information, visit west1jess.com

Daniel Arthur Smith is a USA Today bestselling author. His titles include *Spectral Shift, Hugh Howey Lives, The Cathari Treasure, The Somali Deception*, and a few other novels and short stories. He also curates the phenomenal short fiction series *Tales from the Canyons of the Damned* and *Frontiers of Speculative Fiction*.

He was raised in Michigan and graduated from Western Michigan University where he studied philosophy, with focus on cognitive science, meta-physics, and comparative religion. He began his career as a bartender, barista, poetry house proprietor, teacher, and then became a technologist and futurist for the Fortune 100 across the Americas and Europe.

Daniel has traveled to over 300 cities in 22 countries, residing in Los Angeles, Kalamazoo, Prague, Crete, and now writes in Manhattan where he lives with his wife and young sons.

For more information, visit danielarthursmith.com

www.ingramcontent.com/pod-product-compliance
Lightning Source LLC
Chambersburg PA
CBHW020547130626
46552CB00007B/2789